This edition published by Parragon Books Ltd in 2016

Parragon Books Ltd
Chartist House
15–17 Trim Street
Bath BA1 1HA, UK
www.parragon.com

Disney PRINCESS

STORYBOOK
COLLECTION

PaRragon

Bath · New York · Cologne · Melbourne · Delhi
Hong Kong · Shenzhen · Singapore

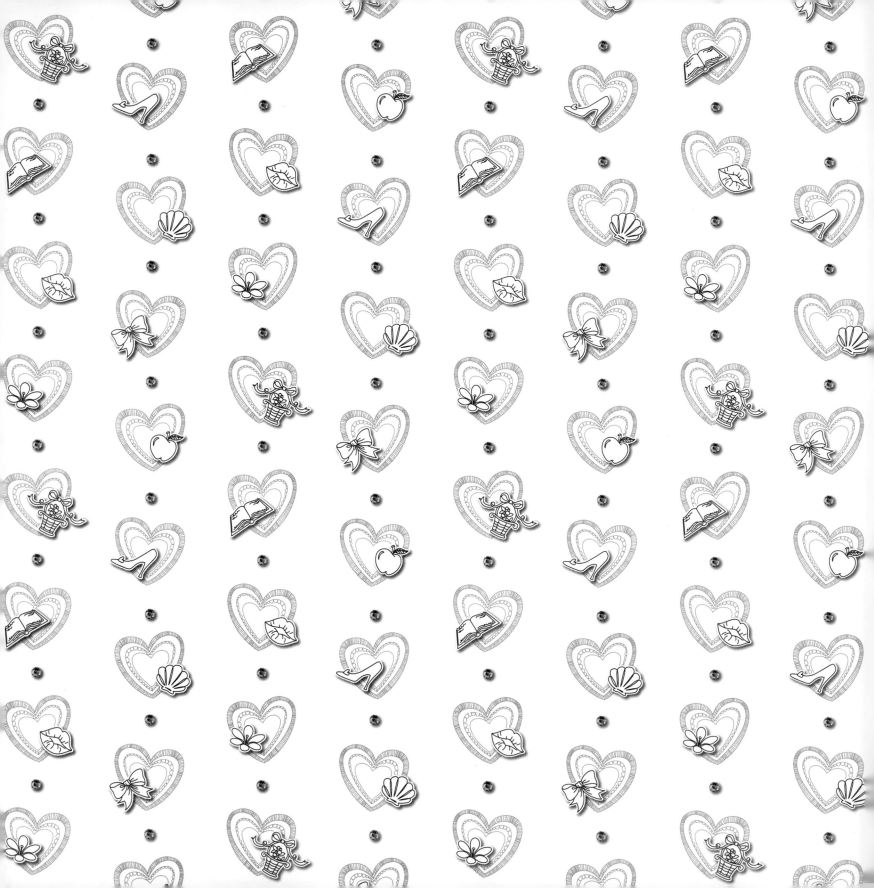

Contents

Tangled

Wanted: Flynn Rider

Princess Rapunzel and Flynn Rider were visiting their friends at the Snuggly Duckling. Rapunzel was being taught how to play the piano by Hook Hand. Flynn was learning interior design. He was less excited than Rapunzel.

"A little to the right," Gunther said.

"The right? Really?" Flynn asked as he moved a vase.

Suddenly, the door flew open. It was the noble horse Max, followed by two royal guards. Max sadly held up a wanted poster in his mouth. It had a picture of Flynn!

"Anyone else getting a sense of déjà vu?" Flynn asked.

"It looks like they think you stole my tiara again," Rapunzel said as she read the warrant for Flynn's arrest.

"What? I didn't do anything! Why does everyone always think it's me?" Flynn said.

Rapunzel just looked at him.

"Well, I guess they might have a few reasons," Flynn said.

The guards explained that late the night before, someone who looked just like Flynn had sneaked into the castle and stolen Rapunzel's tiara, right from under the guards' noses! There were witnesses all over town who said they had seen Flynn running away from the scene of the crime. The guards had no choice but to arrest Flynn.

"Don't worry," Rapunzel said. "We'll clear this whole thing up. You'll be back to interior designing in no time."

"Hurry," Flynn said as the guards led him away. "And don't let Gunther move the vase!"

The door shut behind Max, the guards and Flynn.

"What are we going to do?" Hook Hand asked Rapunzel.

Rapunzel looked at all her friends in the Snuggly Duckling.

She was worried. She knew Flynn hadn't stolen the tiara, but she would have to prove it. "Let's go back to town. It's time to investigate!" Rapunzel said.

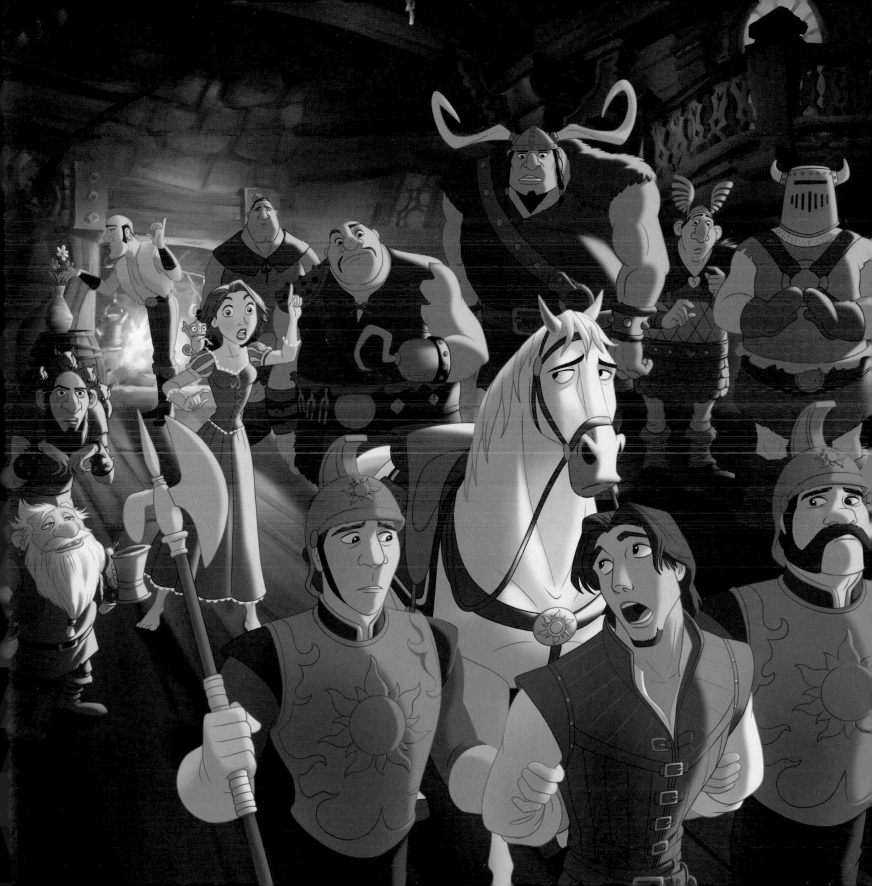

Later that day, Rapunzel and her friends reached Corona and questioned the townspeople. The town was buzzing with news and theories about the theft of the tiara.

"I heard that Flynn Rider stole it to give to a princess from a faraway land," a shopkeeper told Bruiser.

"Oh, please," said Rapunzel.

A baker said that he had heard Flynn was trading the tiara for his freedom from an evil magician. And a gardener said that Flynn was going to use the tiara to buy a ship and sail far, far away.

"He'd never do that," Rapunzel said. "He hates sailing."

Many people swore they had seen Flynn the night before. The librarian had spotted Flynn sneaking around by the paint shop. A sailor was sure he'd seen Flynn down by the docks.

"But how did you know it was him?" Rapunzel asked the sailor.

"The thief was wearing a green waistcoat, just like Flynn always wears," the sailor said matter-of-factly. "Besides, he's stolen the tiara before."

"But he couldn't have been at the paint shop *and* the docks. They're on opposite sides of town, and there aren't two Flynns," Rapunzel said. "Plus, the last time he stole the tiara, he had some extra help...."

Rapunzel turned to her friends. She was starting to suspect who might *really* be behind the theft. But to clear Flynn's name, they would have to catch the true criminals.

"I think I have a plan," Rapunzel said, drawing everyone into a tight huddle. "Now, listen closely...."

Rapunzel and her friends rushed to the castle to tell the King and Queen her plan.

"First I need the royal messengers to tell the town we're moving all the royal jewels to the throne room to protect them," Rapunzel said. "Then I need you to send Max and all his guards on an important mission out of town."

"But then everyone will know that the castle and all the jewels are undefended!" said the King and Queen together.

"Exactly." Rapunzel smiled.

The sun began to set, and the townspeople watched in amazement as Max led all his guards out of the city gates.

"They must be going to find the princess's tiara!" the gardener told the town librarian.

The royal messengers told everyone that the kingdom's jewels had all been moved to the castle's throne room. With everything in one place, the precious treasure would be easier to protect.

"Especially from evil magicians," the baker told the gardener.

Soon it was time for everyone in the castle to go to sleep. It had been a long, eventful day, and everyone was tired. Without any of the guards in the castle, there was no one to notice two shadowy figures crawling over the roof. And there were no guards to see those same two figures lower a rope into the dark throne room and slowly climb down. The thieves were back to steal the royal jewels! They softly landed on the floor of the throne room.

Then quietly walked towards the centre of the room, looking for the royal jewels. But the room was empty!

"I don't understand," said a gruff voice. "Where are all the jewels?"

Suddenly, the room was full of light. Rapunzel and her friends ran out of their hiding place. It had been a trap all along!

In the harsh light of her lantern, Rapunzel saw that the thieves were dressed in matching green waistcoats – just like Flynn's. But she wasn't fooled for a moment. As Atilla and Hook Hand restrained the criminals, Rapunzel removed their brown wigs to reveal ... the Stabbington brothers!

"How did you know we'd be here?" one of the brothers asked Rapunzel.

"I knew that the idea of getting more jewels would be too tempting for you to pass up," Rapunzel said. "Especially when you had seen all the guards leave the city. You didn't know that I had a scary group of thugs to help me out!"

Rapunzel explained to her friends how the Stabbington brothers had disguised themselves as Flynn to hide their true identities. That was why the townspeople had seen Flynn in so many different places. There *had* been two of him!

"We knew that you would get to the bottom of this, Rapunzel," the Queen said, giving her daughter a hug.

Rapunzel smiled. "Now, if you'll excuse me, I have some business in the dungeon...."

With Flynn's name cleared, Max and Rapunzel freed him from jail.

"I left the room warm for you," Flynn told the thieves as Hook Hand and Vladimir locked them up.

Now there was only one mystery left to solve. "Where is my tiara?" Rapunzel asked the Stabbington brothers. "I can get my frying pan if I have to!"

"Boys, I'd be careful," Flynn said. "You do not want to be on the wrong end of Rapunzel's frying pan. Believe me. I know."

"It's right here!" said one of the brothers, pulling the tiara from beneath his waistcoat. "After we stole all the jewels, we were planning to go to the docks and sail away to a faraway land."

"Not any more," Flynn said as he took the tiara and placed it on Rapunzel's head. "That's better."

To celebrate solving the mystery, everyone went back to the Snuggly Duckling for a 'Welcome Back' party.

"Be honest, you were a little nervous," Rapunzel said to Flynn.

"Me? Nervous? Never! I'm Flynn Rider. I've sailed to distant lands to see fair princesses and battled evil magicians. Adventure is my life!" Flynn said with a wink.

"Good thing, too," Gunther said. "Because you're a terrible interior designer."

Rapunzel laughed. It was good to be among friends.

The End

The Secret of the Star Shell

"Do, re, mi, fa, so, la, ti, do!"

"Very good, Laurel!" Princess Ariel applauded.

It was a bright and sunny morning in the village. Ariel was giving her young friend Laurel a singing lesson.

"Why don't we try this one next?" Ariel pointed to a song in her music book.

Laurel's eyes sparkled. "'The Song of the Sea' – that reminds me of my new best friend!"

"What's your friend's name?" Ariel asked.

Laurel suddenly hesitated. "Um, I'm not sure you'd know her. But we love playing together." She glanced at the clock. "I'm meeting her right after our lesson. Maybe I'll sing 'The Song of the Sea' for her, too!"

Later that afternoon, Ariel visited her sisters by the sea.

"Ariel!" Adella sang out. "We brought you a present!"

She handed Ariel a shimmering shell shaped like a star. It had a delicate ribbon tied to the top.

"Oh, it's beautiful!" Ariel gasped. "Where did you find it?"

"It was caught in the current," Adella explained. "It's a star shell. It's supposed to grant wishes!"

Ariel looked at her sisters excitedly.

"Shall we try it?"

They each took turns making one wish, but nothing happened.

"That's all right," Ariel said. She tied the ribbon round her neck to wear the shell like a necklace. "It's a beautiful gift. Now I'll carry a part of the sea wherever I go."

As Ariel walked back to the village, she passed Laurel's cottage. Suddenly, Laurel's father, Mr Hansen, came running out.

"Princess Ariel! Is Laurel with you?" He sounded upset.

"No," said Ariel. "Has something happened?"

"Laurel went to play with a friend after your music lesson, but she never came back," Mr Hansen explained. "I checked with all her school friends. Laurel isn't with any of them. I hope she hasn't got lost."

"Laurel mentioned that she'd made a new friend," Ariel said. "Maybe they're still playing and they lost track of time. Perhaps there's a clue in her room about who this friend is and where we could find her."

Together, they checked the girl's room. Scattered on Laurel's desk were school drawings and a pink journal open to an entry:

Dear Diary,

I met a new friend by the sea. Her name is Calista! We've played together every day this week. She even gave me a beautiful necklace. Calista said not to tell anyone about our secret friendship. But that's okay — it's fun having a secret friend. I'm going to buy her a treat from the pastry shop!

Ariel and Mr Hansen agreed to split up and search for Laurel. Mr Hansen went to ask the village parents if they knew Calista. Ariel hurried to the pastry shop.

"Hmmm," the baker said, when Ariel explained what had happened. "Yes, I do remember Laurel stopping by. She wanted seaweed puffs! Can you imagine?"

Just then, a little girl named Maggie bounded into the bakery with her mother. She handed the baker a colourful card.

He smiled. "Why, it's a thank-you note!"

"It was part of a school assignment," Maggie's mother told the baker. "Miss Toft asked the students to write them, and Maggie wanted to thank you for her birthday cake."

Ariel looked thoughtful. Miss Toft was Laurel's teacher, too. That meant Laurel would have had the same assignment. Perhaps she wrote a thank-you note to Calista for the necklace, and it would hold another clue!

Thank you for baking my yummy birthday cake! Your friend Maggie

At the school, the teacher was happy to show Ariel the thank-you notes. Laurel's was written on a bright yellow card.

Dear Princess Ariel,

Thank you for helping me practise singing.

Your friend, Laurel

"Oh, dear." Ariel sighed. The card was lovely, but it certainly wasn't a clue.

"Laurel loves drawing," the teacher said. "Just yesterday, I asked my students to make a picture of their best friend. Laurel couldn't wait to get started."

"Best friend?" Ariel exclaimed. "Maybe she drew a picture of Calista!"

My best friend

Laurel

Miss Toft took Ariel to Laurel's desk. "Surely the picture is in here somewhere."

After looking through a few folders, Ariel found a picture labelled 'My best friend'.

Two girls were in the drawing. One was Laurel, with short brown hair. And the other girl had wavy blonde hair. It had to be Calista. And she was a mermaid!

Ariel thanked Miss Toft and ran back to Mr Hansen's home.

Mr Hansen looked up hopefully when he spotted Ariel. "Princess! None of the parents knew a Calista. Did you have better luck?"

"Yes!" Ariel exclaimed. She quickly told Mr Hansen what she had discovered.

"Could Calista really be a mermaid?" Mr Hansen asked.

"It does make sense," Ariel said. "Look at the clues. Laurel met her by the sea. She tried to buy her seaweed puffs. And Calista wanted to keep their friendship a secret. She must be a mermaid!"

"But then where is my daughter?" Mr Hansen asked.

Ariel smiled. "I think I know how to find out!"

Ariel led Mr Hansen to the beach and called for her friends Sebastian and Flounder. Ariel asked them to fetch her father, King Triton, so he could transform her back into a mermaid. In no time at all, Ariel was searching for Calista under the sea.

After asking the merfolk, Ariel and her father found Calista's family's grotto.

The young mermaid was there. And she was very nervous.

"You're not in trouble," Ariel assured Calista. "We just want to know where Laurel is. Her father is very worried."

"I don't want anyone to worry," Calista said softly. She led Ariel and Triton to her bedroom.

"It's all right," Calista called. "You can come out."

Slowly, Laurel swam out from under Calista's bed.

Ariel gasped. "Laurel! You're here! And ... you're a mermaid, too?"

"It's so hard to explain." Laurel cried. "When I went to see Calista this morning, I was wearing my star shell necklace. As we were splashing in the water, I told Calista that I wished I could play with her under the sea for real. All of a sudden, my necklace lit up. And I turned into a mermaid!"

Calista nodded. "We realized the shell must be magical. So we thought we could just wish Laurel to be human again later."

"But while we were playing on the octopus slide," Laurel said, "my necklace got swept away in a current. I didn't know what to do!"

Suddenly, Calista spotted Ariel's star shell necklace. "Oh, Princess! You found it! That means we can wish Laurel human again!"

Ariel looked to her father. King Triton smiled kindly.

"I'm afraid the Legend of the Star Shell works a little differently," he said. "Come with me to the surface, and I'll explain."

At the surface, King Triton held up the star shell. It glittered in the sunlight.

"Star shells can only grant one wish," he said. "In order to undo the wish, the shell must be broken."

Calista turned to Laurel. "When you're human again, will you still visit me by the sea?"

"Of course!" Laurel said with a smile.

Together, everyone swam back to shore. Then Ariel handed Laurel the star shell. "It's up to you now."

Laurel lifted the shell high up in the air, paused, and then brought it down against a large flat rock. In a burst of light, her mermaid tail changed back into legs.

"I'm human!" Laurel cried. She hugged Calista tightly. "It was a wonderful adventure. We'll still see each other all the time. I promise."

Immediately, Mr Hansen rushed over. "Laurel! Thank goodness you're safe!"

"Oh, Daddy!" Laurel cried. "I have so much to tell you."

A few days later, Ariel asked Calista and Laurel to meet her by the water.

"I have presents for you both," Ariel said. She handed the girls two brand-new necklaces made from star shell pieces.

"They're really beautiful!" Laurel breathed.

"Thank you, Princess Ariel," Calista said.

Ariel smiled. "When I was wearing the star shell, it was like carrying a part of the sea with me. Now you two can always carry a piece of your adventure with you wherever you go."

A New Mouse

W arm sunlight streamed through the windows of Cinderella's parlour as she and her mouse friends shared afternoon tea.

Even though the food was delicious, Cinderella found it difficult to enjoy the tasty treats. She was too busy thinking about her friend Gabrielle, who would be visiting very soon. Gabrielle was the Prince's cousin, but she lived so far away that Cinderella didn't get to see her very often.

Just then, a royal page entered the parlour. "Lady Gabrielle has arrived," he announced. Gabrielle swept into the room and ran to hug Cinderella.

"It's so good to see you, dear," she said. As the two friends chatted excitedly, Jaq and Gus noticed that Gabrielle had an unusual item with her.

"What's-a that?" Jaq said. He pointed eagerly to a fancy little house that Gabrielle had set on the floor.

Gabrielle noticed the curious mice and explained right away.

"Let me introduce you to my beloved friend Babette." Gabrielle opened the little door to the house, and Babette walked onto her hand.

Jaq and Gus couldn't believe it. Babette was a mouse!

"I found little Babette lost in one of the manor bedrooms," Gabrielle said. "After meeting your mouse friends, Cinderella, I just knew I had to take her in."

Jaq and Gus waved to the new mouse, but Babette just stared at them.

"Would you like a crumpet, Babette?" Cinderella asked.

The mouse took a piece and ran back onto Gabrielle's hand.

"She should-a said 'thank-a you'," Jaq whispered to Gus.

"Rude!" Gus agreed.

"Cinderella, dear, you simply must show me the castle garden," Gabrielle said, setting down Babette.

"Jaq, Gus, perhaps you can give Babette a tour of the castle," Cinderella suggested.

Jaq and Gus agreed and
immediately began showing Babette
all their favourite places in the castle.
"This-a the library!" Jaq said.

"Lots-a books," Gus said, pointing.
Babette looked around but didn't
say a word.

Then Jaq and Gus took Babette
to the grand ballroom. "You have a
ballroom?" Jaq asked, trying to start
a conversation.

Babette nodded. And that
was all.

Jaq and Gus took Babette all over the castle, hoping to find something that she would be interested in. But no matter where they went, Babette just nodded or stayed silent.

That evening, Cinderella asked Jaq and Gus how their day with Babette had been.

"She's a snob," Jaq told Cinderella.

"Stuck up!" Gus agreed.

"Now, now," Cinderella said gently. "You hardly know her. Give her a chance."

As Cinderella set the pair of mice down on the ground, she noticed something was missing. "My bracelet!" she gasped. "It must have fallen off during Gabrielle's tour."

"We can find it, Cinderelly!" Jaq said.

"Oh, thank you for offering," Cinderella said, "but we went all over the castle. The bracelet could be anywhere."

"No problem for Jaq and Gus-Gus!" Jaq said very proudly. "Just follow us, Cinderelly!"

They went to ask Gabrielle about the last time she remembered seeing the bracelet.

"Oh, dear. I'm afraid I was so busy admiring the castle that I wasn't paying much attention to Cinderella's bracelet," Gabrielle said.

"I can help you look," a soft voice said. It was Babette, stepping out from her little house.

Jaq and Gus looked suspiciously at Babette, but Cinderella spoke up for her. "That would be wonderful. Thank you, Babette."

Jaq reluctantly agreed. "We check the mouse-size places, and Cinderelly check the princess-size places."

The three mice scurried from room to room.
They looked behind curtains, on top of cabinets,
and even in the tea room. Gus checked inside
an entire tea set.

"Gus-Gus, Cinderelly's bracelet isn't in
a teapot," Jaq laughed.

Gus looked embarrassed, but Babette spoke up quietly. "It never
hurts to check."

The mice continued searching
the tea room until Babette let out a
squeal of joy.

"Jaq! Gus! Look!" she cried.
Babette had found Cinderella's
bracelet stuck between two
chair cushions.

"Hooray!" Gus and Jaq cheered.

The pair of mice hopped down to help Babette free the heavy bracelet from between the cushions.

"You can tell Cinderelly you found it!" Gus said.

"Oh, I couldn't!" Babette said, blushing.

Suddenly, Jaq and Gus understood why Babette had been so quiet. Babette wasn't a snob. She was just shy!

"Be brave!" Gus said, patting her on the shoulder.

"Cinderelly is the nicest princess ever," Jaq said. "You can talk to her."

The mice found Cinderella looking through her bedroom.

Jaq and Gus gently pushed Babette forward with the bracelet.

"Oh, you little dear!" Cinderella cried. "Did you find my bracelet?"

Babette blushed and nodded.

"Thank you," Cinderella said.

Babette saw that she was surrounded by kind friends. She gathered all her courage, looked Cinderella in the eye, and said, "You're welcome, Princess."

Now that the bracelet had been found, the three mice decided to play together. Gus had a wonderful idea. He grabbed Babette's paw.

"Hide-and-seek!" he squeaked.

The three friends ran off together. They spent the rest of the day playing in the many castle rooms they had explored earlier.

But their fun couldn't last forever. When it was time for Gabrielle to go home, Jaq and Gus were very sorry to say goodbye to their new friend.

"Come back soon!" Gus said.

Babette waved. "I'll miss you!" she said.

Cinderella, Jaq and Gus walked outside to see the carriage off. When Gabrielle and Babette were out of sight, Jaq turned to Cinderella.

"Babette!" he said. "She's so much fun."

"The best!" Gus chimed in.

"Oh, really?" Cinderella asked with a smile. "She's not 'stuck up' or a 'snob'?"

"We're sorry, Cinderelly," Jaq said.

"That's all right, Jaq," Cinderella replied. "I'm sure you'll be more patient with new friends in the future."

Gus nodded sagely, while Jaq exclaimed, "We sure will!"

DISNEY PRINCESS

Tangled

The Sweetest Day Ever

Rapunzel was having the best birthday of her life. She'd finally left her tower. She and her chameleon, Pascal, had made some new friends – like Flynn, the well-meaning thief, and Maximus, the noble horse. In a few short hours, she'd get to see the floating lanterns she'd always wondered about.

And now they had time to explore the kingdom of Corona.
Since today was the celebration of the lost princess's birthday, the
whole town was out and about for the festivities.

Rapunzel had never met so many interesting people. There were musicians playing lively tunes, kids drawing with chalk, and all sorts of street vendors selling goodies. Rapunzel found she had plenty to talk about with all of them.

"Hello there!" called a man behind a fruit stand. "Crispy, delicious apples? They're straight from my farm."

Rapunzel bounded up to greet him. "They certainly look delicious," she responded. "What's it like owning a farm?"

Farther down the street, Rapunzel got into a conversation with another vendor. "Wow! Are these your paintings? What types of brushes do you use?"

"I know a fellow artist when I see one," the painter said. The two started chatting like old friends.

Suddenly, Rapunzel and Flynn heard a commotion behind them. The sounds of crashing pans and loud voices erupted from an open window.

"I have half a mind to call the palace guards!" a voice cried.

"Hey! A bakery!" Rapunzel said, noticing the sign. She headed straight for the door.

"Um ... what was that about 'palace guards'?" Flynn asked. He knew the guards weren't that good at hunting him down, but he didn't want to walk straight to them. "Besides, I don't even like sweets!"

Despite Flynn's protests, Rapunzel followed her curiosity inside.
Her attention was immediately drawn to the lively feud in front of her.

"I'm sorry, but we're all out!" said a small man crouching in fear.

"How can you be out on today of all days?" a flushed baker
asked the dairyman. "How am I going to make my famous Lost
Princess Cupcakes without milk and eggs?"

Rapunzel stepped forward. "Wait, you don't have eggs or milk?"

"That's right," the baker responded, her eyes narrowing at the strange blonde girl who'd suddenly appeared in front of her.

"I can help! Stay right there," Rapunzel declared. And with that, she ran out of the bakery as fast as she could.

The baker and the dairyman now turned to stare at the man left standing awkwardly nearby.

"Uh ... I guess I'll go and help," Flynn said, darting out after her.

First, Rapunzel rushed back to the farmer's stand. Flynn, Maximus and Pascal hurried after her.

"Hi again, Frank! I need some of your finest!" Rapunzel grabbed as many apples as she could carry.

Then they stopped by the artist's corner. "You don't have any unused paintbrushes you could spare, do you, Felix?" Rapunzel asked.

Soon girl, boy, horse and chameleon were back at the bakery, their goods in tow.

The baker led Rapunzel into the kitchen, curious about what the girl was going to propose. She was so intrigued she didn't even think twice about the large horse and bright chameleon peeking into her shop.

"You don't need eggs or milk," Rapunzel announced, pulling out some pots and pans from behind the counter. "You can use applesauce!"

"Applesauce?" repeated the baker.

"Yep!" Rapunzel taught the baker her favourite way of whipping up some applesauce quickly.

In no time, golden, fluffy cupcakes were cooling on the counter.

"And now to add a little pizzazz," Rapunzel said. She grabbed one of the borrowed paintbrushes and started to decorate the cupcakes with colourful icing. The baker inspected Rapunzel's work with admiration.

"You saved the day!" the baker said. "Cupcakes for everyone ... even you, Lester," she said, eyeing the dairyman. She handed Flynn a basket filled with the beautiful sweet treats.

Rapunzel and Flynn knew just where to take them. Saving the Lost Princess Cupcakes had been a team effort, after all.

Frank loved the sweet taste.

Felix loved the icing decorations.

"I think I'll try one now, too," Rapunzel said, taking a cupcake out of the basket.

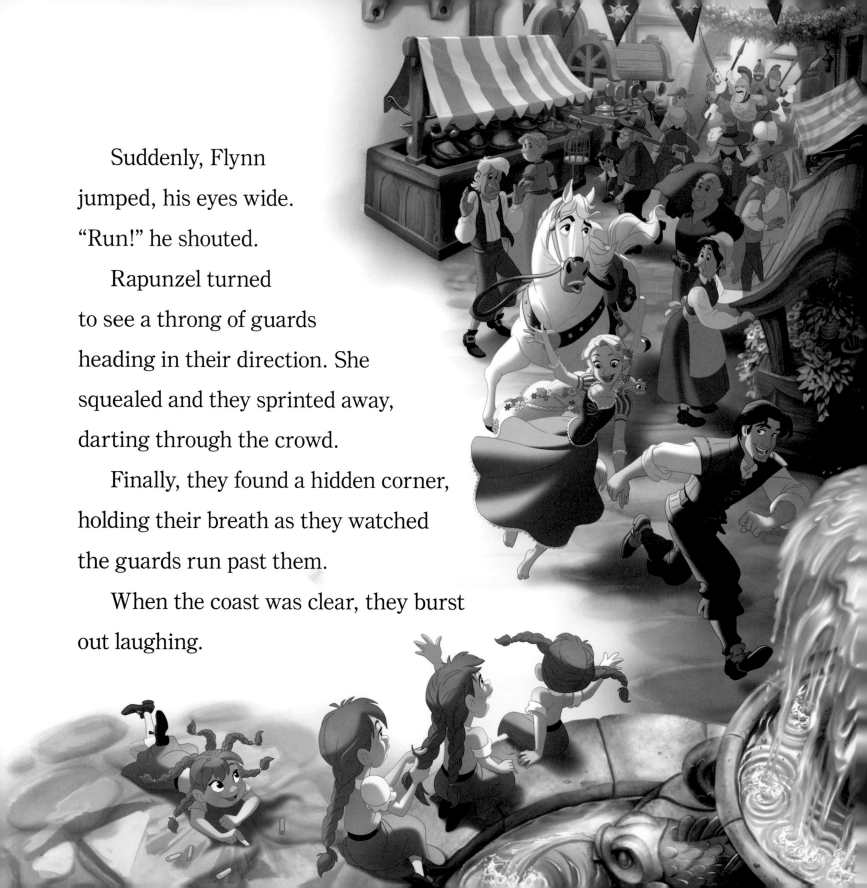

Suddenly, Flynn
jumped, his eyes wide.
"Run!" he shouted.

Rapunzel turned
to see a throng of guards
heading in their direction. She
squealed and they sprinted away,
darting through the crowd.

Finally, they found a hidden corner,
holding their breath as they watched
the guards run past them.

When the coast was clear, they burst
out laughing.

"I sure have worked up an appetite," Flynn said, grabbing a cupcake from the basket.

"I thought you didn't like sweets," Rapunzel teased.

"I'll make an exception this time," he said, tipping his cupcake towards Rapunzel and taking a bite. "Wow! That *is* delicious."

"Thanks," Rapunzel said, taking a bite out of her own. They looked at each other for a moment and both felt themselves blushing and grinning.

As the sun started to set, Rapunzel thought about how truly sweet the day had been ... and it wasn't over yet! Soon it would be time to see the floating lanterns with her best friends at her side.

BRAVE

The Legend of the Emeralds

Princess Merida raced down the palace hallway. She had looked forward to the Rites of Summer all year long! It was a special festival that celebrated the friendship between the clans. This year, the Macintosh clan would be her family's honoured guests. There would be dancing, games and feats of strength!

At the docks, everyone gathered to greet their visitors.

Young Macintosh stepped down from the boat. The sunlight glinted off a family crest tied to his kilt sash.

"Oh, fancy, are we?" Merida teased him.

Young Macintosh grinned. "What, you don't have a crest of your own?"

"No – but I have this," Merida replied, showing him a lucky charm tied to her bow. "So, shall I beat you at archery or to the top of the Fire Falls first?" she challenged with a sly smile.

"To the Fire Falls!" Young Macintosh cried.

Merida jumped on her horse, Angus, and Young Macintosh followed close behind.

The two reached the base of the Fire Falls at the same time. They began to climb the craggy rocks. They were neck and neck as they approached the top.

Merida pulled herself up. "I won!" she cried.

"Barely!" argued Young Macintosh. Then he looked around. "Wow, this is a fine waterfall you've got here," he remarked. "Where does all this water come from?"

"I'm not sure," Merida replied. "Let's find out!"

Merida and Young Macintosh walked deeper into the forest. Then they stopped short at the edge of a deep lake.

"I suppose this is it," Merida said, disappointed. "I fancied we would have an adventure, but this is just a common loch." She tried climbing a boulder to get a better view. Suddenly, the boulder moved! Merida stumbled forwards into a cave, and Young Macintosh jumped up to follow her.

When Merida caught her balance, she gasped at what they found.

"It's the *real* source of the Fire Falls!" Merida exclaimed, pointing at a pool of glowing water. There, two large, glowing emeralds were resting on a stone ledge. "Those emeralds must be lucky!" she said.

"*Lucky?*" Young Macintosh asked. "But emeralds are a symbol of power, not luck."

"Everyone knows emeralds bring good luck!" Merida scoffed.

Merida and Young Macintosh began to argue.

Suddenly, Young Macintosh snatched up one of the emeralds. "I'm taking this to my father. *Then* you'll see how powerful emeralds are. The Macintosh clan will be stronger than ever!"

"Then I'll be taking the other one!" Merida exclaimed.

They each put an emerald in their own pouch. Neither one noticed that the gems had stopped glowing.

Back at the castle, Lord Macintosh assured them that the emerald was a symbol of power.

"Lord Macintosh is correct," replied Queen Elinor. "But it also symbolizes luck. And we sometimes forget the emerald's most *important* meaning: loyalty. The ancient Legend of the Emeralds is why we're here today." She explained that there used to be fighting between the clans. Then two great kings rose to power, and each placed an emerald at the source of the Fire Falls to symbolize their clans' new friendship. As long as the Fire Falls ran sparkling, there would be peace.

Suddenly, a DunBroch clansman raced into the hall. "The Fire Falls – they've gone dark!" he cried.

Everyone raced outside to look at the lifeless falls. "Who has done this?" cried King Fergus.

Lord Macintosh nodded. "Yes, when King Fergus finds out which one of his DunBroch clansmen did this, he will have my support."

"Which one of *my* clansmen? It was probably one of *your* clansmen," King Fergus said.

The men glared at each other.

"Macintosh clan!" Lord Macintosh commanded. "We're leaving!"

Merida and Young Macintosh looked at each other as everyone else went back to the castle. They *had* to get those emeralds back to where they belonged before the friendship between their clans was ruined! The pair tried to climb up to the cave, but the new, darkened water made the rocks too slippery.

Suddenly, Merida saw a blue will-o'-the-wisp! She knew it would lead them to their destiny. More wisps appeared, drawing Merida's eyes to the top of the falls, where she noticed a small tree.

"If only we had a rope ..." Merida said.

"You mean, like this?" Young Macintosh asked, showing her a long coil. "I'll throw it up so it twists round that tree," he suggested. But he couldn't throw far enough.

Then Merida had an idea. She picked out her strongest arrow and attached the rope. She pulled back the bowstring, adjusted her aim, and – *WHOOSH!* – the arrow flew into the sky and landed next to the tree.

Carefully, Merida used the
rope to climb the rocks. When
she was at the top, she tied
the rope to the tree. Young
Macintosh followed her up.
He was almost at the top when
the rope suddenly snapped!

Young Macintosh began to
fall, but he grabbed on to a rock
just in time. Merida reached out
to give him a hand. As she did,
her pouch tipped forward, and
the emerald she had carefully
tucked inside plunged over
the cliff!

"No!" Merida cried. The emerald was gone. Merida helped Young Macintosh up.

"You saved my life!" he said. "Thank you."

Merida and Young Macintosh didn't know what they would do, but they hurried back to the cave. The water of the Fire Falls was getting even darker. When they reached the cave, Young Macintosh tried to put the emerald back where he had found it. It nearly toppled off the stone ledge!

Merida looked concerned.

"The two emeralds must have supported each other," she said.

What were they going to do without the other stone?

"The legend!" Merida suddenly gasped. "Each king put an emerald on the stone. We've got to put something there, too!" She removed her lucky charm from her bow and placed it on the ledge.

Young Macintosh placed a small knife. For a moment, a sparkling flash crackled and there was a burst of light. But it quickly faded.

Merida shook her head. "It can't just be anything. It has to be something that really, truly matters."

Young Macintosh nodded. He carefully unpinned his family's crest from his kilt sash and placed it on the ledge.

A halo of green light surrounded the objects as they lit up with dazzling sparkles. A golden light flickered out from under the ledge, filling the whole cave.

Then, finally, the water began to glow again! Merida and Young Macintosh raced from the cave just in time to see the Fire Falls turn from black into a clear crystal blue.

From the top of the falls, Merida and Young Macintosh could see the docks. There, clan Macintosh was preparing to leave!

Merida picked out her father, who was standing next to Lord Macintosh. "They're probably still shouting at each other," she said with a heavy sigh.

Quickly, Merida and Young Macintosh raced back down the falls and rode towards the dock.

"Wait!" Young Macintosh called when they were close enough. "We don't have to leave!"

"The Fire Falls are sparkling again," Merida cried. "The water flows as beautifully as it always has!" She explained how she and Young Macintosh had been the ones responsible for ruining the falls – and for fixing them again.

"Now there's no reason our clans can't stay friends," Merida finished hopefully.

"So we don't have to leave?" Young Macintosh asked his father.

King Fergus and Lord Macintosh looked at each other.

"Of course not!" exclaimed Lord Macintosh, smiling at King Fergus.

Merida and Young Macintosh also shared a smile. By working together, they had fixed the Fire Falls – and the argument between their clans. From then on, the Rites of Summer would have a special meaning for both of them.

Aladdin

The Search for the Sultan's Stone

The sun shone brightly in the sky. Jasmine surveyed the palace grounds. There was still work to do! Tomorrow was the Day of Unity – the day each year when all of Agrabah celebrated the city's history. And this year was the 500th anniversary!

Nearby, she spotted her father, the Sultan, speaking excitedly to one of their servants. Jasmine moved closer to listen.

The servant, Farid, shook his head. "I'm sorry, Sultan, but the search party failed to find the stone. The Halari Jungle is just too vast."

The Sultan looked very disappointed. "Thank you for letting me know."

The Halari Jungle? Jasmine thought. She'd always wanted to go there, but her father said it was too dangerous. She found Aladdin and told him what she had heard.

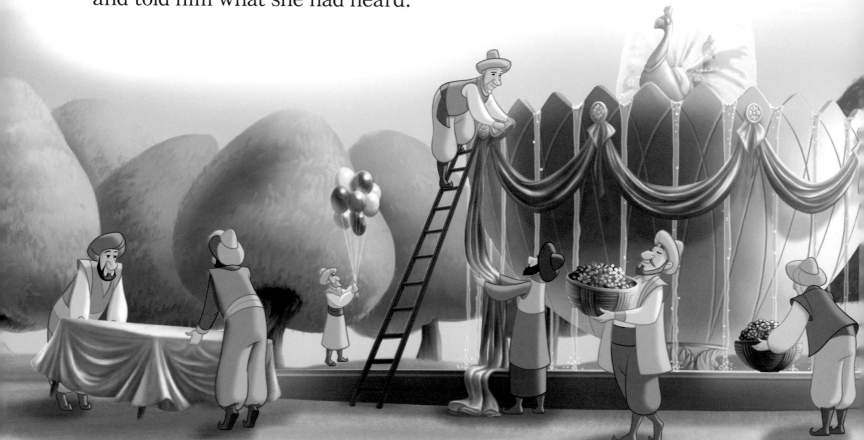

"I bet he was talking about the Sultan's Stone," Aladdin said. "The first sultan of Agrabah was beloved by all. But the sultan's brother was jealous. So he stole an important stone that belonged to the sultan and hid it behind a waterfall in the jungle. No one has ever been able to find it."

"Until today," Jasmine said. "Because *we're* going to find it."

"Sounds like my kind of adventure," Aladdin replied.

He whistled for the Magic Carpet and Abu, and together they took off for the Halari Jungle.

On the way, Jasmine asked Aladdin more about the stone. "What does the Sultan's Stone look like, exactly?"

"Most people believe it's a statue of the first sultan. No one knows what he looked like. I wonder if –"

"That's it!" Jasmine interrupted, pointing to a dense forest in the middle of the desert. "The Halari Jungle!" The Magic Carpet glided to the ground right on the edge of the jungle. Jasmine told the Magic Carpet that they'd return soon.

Jasmine led the way. The jungle was beautiful. It didn't seem scary at all! *Why was Father so concerned about me coming here?* she wondered. *It's so peaceful and –*

"Jasmine, look out!" Aladdin cried.

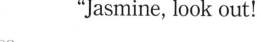

Jasmine stopped just in time. They were at the edge of a swamp!

Abu squeaked wildly and pointed. Something was moving in the swamp. And not just anything – it was a crocodile!

"Uh ... maybe we should turn around and try a different route," Aladdin suggested.

But Jasmine spotted just what they needed – two long, strong branches. She handed Aladdin one of the branches. With the other, she vaulted clear over the swamp!

Aladdin used his branch to cross over after her. "Nice work, Princess," he told her. "Now let's find this thing and get out of here."

After just a few steps, they came to a clearing. In the centre was a giant stone covered with beautiful jewels. "Well, that was easy," Aladdin said, giving Jasmine a quizzical look. Could this be the Sultan's Stone? Jasmine started to walk towards the stone, but Aladdin stopped her.

"Jasmine, if the stone is right here, why has no one discovered it yet?" he said. "And I don't see any waterfalls around here."

"Good point," Jasmine replied. "It could be a trap." Instead of walking closer to the stone herself, Jasmine picked a grapefruit from a nearby tree and rolled it to the base of the stone.

ZAP! As soon as the grapefruit hit the stone, there was a blinding burst of light. The grapefruit instantly burned to cinders. Jasmine gasped. "The sultan's brother must have been a powerful enchanter to make a stone do that."

"Well, I'm glad the grapefruit found that out the hard way, and not us!" Aladdin replied.

Jasmine thought the trap must mean they were heading in the right direction. But after hours of searching, she started to wonder if Aladdin had been right. Maybe they *should* have tried a different route to begin with. Everyone was tired, hungry and ready for a rest. When Jasmine turned round to suggest a break, she saw that Abu had a bunch of berries in his hand. They were a beautiful purple colour and they looked exactly like ...

"Abu!" Jasmine cried as Abu popped a few berries into his mouth. "Those are Nightbloom berries. They're poisonous!"

Abu squeaked and spat out the berries.

"It's a good thing you didn't eat those, Abu!" Aladdin said. "I know you're hungry. We'll get you dinner soon."

But the berries had got Jasmine thinking. Nightbloom berries only grew near water. Jasmine raced ahead, and sure enough, there it was! The waterfall!

Aladdin and Abu caught up. "You found it!" Aladdin cried.

Jasmine and Aladdin walked over to get a closer look. A path of mossy rocks led right behind the falls. Eagerly, Jasmine stepped onto the first rock – and almost slipped into the rushing water!

Slowly, they made it across. But when they reached the back of the waterfall, there was only a bare cave wall! Jasmine sighed. Had they come all this way for nothing? She leaned against the wall to rest. Suddenly, the wall *moved*. "Aladdin, help me push this open!" she exclaimed.

They pushed with all their strength. Slowly but surely, the wall began to turn. When it was fully open, Jasmine and Aladdin saw that there was a secret room!

In the centre of the room sat an ancient wooden box. But Jasmine and Aladdin didn't reach for it right away. They remembered what had happened with the stone trap!

Aladdin scanned the room. He took one step forward, lightly placing his foot on the floor. Immediately, the floor tiles began to crumble beneath the pressure. "Jasmine," he said, "are you ready to run? Fast?"

Jasmine nodded, and together they bolted for the pedestal. As the pair ran, the entire floor crumbled behind them! Loose rocks began to fall from above. They dodged left, then right, and just as Aladdin and Jasmine were about to run out of floor, they reached the pedestal.

Instantly, the shaking stopped.

"So, that could have gone better," Aladdin said as he looked at the collapsed cavern behind them.

"At least we have the stone," Jasmine replied, picking up the box. Now empty, the pedestal sank into the ground, revealing a secret passageway.

"Of course! This must be how the sultan's brother escaped after hiding the stone," Jasmine said. They followed the passage down and around, left and right, until they emerged back in the jungle on the other side of the waterfall.

"We made it!" Jasmine cried.

"I think it's time to take a look at that stone," Aladdin said.

Jasmine opened the box, expecting to find a statue covered in precious rubies or sparkling emeralds inside. Instead, she found a very simple carving of a woman wearing royal robes. Jasmine turned it over in her hands.

"Look, there's some writing on it," Aladdin pointed out.

Jasmine peered closely at the writing. "'The Stone of Lilah, the first ruler of Agrabah'," she read. "I guess the first sultan of Agrabah was actually a sultana."

Aladdin smiled. "This is a beautiful statue," he said, admiring it. "And I'm sure Agrabah will be very happy to have it back. Speaking of which ... *we* should probably get back."

At noon the next day, the people of Agrabah gathered in front of the palace.

"Before we celebrate, my daughter would like to speak," the Sultan announced.

Jasmine stepped forward. "We are so excited to have you at the palace," she began. "And we are even *more* excited because we are celebrating something special on this 500th Day of Unity." She thrust the Sultan's Stone into the air. "The return of the Sultan's Stone!" she cried.

The crowd gasped ... and then broke into wild cheers.

Jasmine glanced at her father, whose mouth was wide open.

"But – but how did you find the Sultan's Stone? I thought it was in the Halari Jungle," he said incredulously.

"It *was* in the jungle," Jasmine said with a smile. "I'll take you there sometime." She winked.

The Day of Unity was a huge success. The people of Agrabah packed the palace grounds, eating, playing and, most of all, celebrating the return of the Sultan's Stone.

The Heart
of a Champion

One day, Cinderella was visiting her old friend Frou in the royal stable, when her mouse friends Jaq and Gus told her that a messenger had arrived at the palace! Cinderella said goodbye to Frou and the other horses, and hurried off to hear the news.

It seemed there was going to be a horse show. The King usually entered it, but he never did very well. Now that Cinderella was part of the family, he thought she would be the perfect person to represent them.

"Why, I'd be delighted," Cinderella said when the King suggested it.

The next thing Cinderella knew, the King was leading her back to the royal stable. The Prince and the Grand Duke went with them.

"The finest horsewoman in the kingdom must have the finest horse in the kingdom," the King said. "I have a stable full of champions, my dear. We'll choose the best of the best, and you can begin training right away. Ah, yes! I can see those red ribbons already!"

The King ordered his groomsmen to saddle up his horses – all 122 of them – and bring them out to the courtyard.

Cinderella climbed onto the back of the first horse. She knew the stallion was the King's favourite. But he was just a bit too small. The next horse, however, was too big.

Cinderella sat on one horse after another, but none of them was quite right.

Finally, Cinderella dashed back into the stable. "I'll be right back!" she called. "I know the perfect horse!"

Moments later, Cinderella returned, leading Frou!

The King stared at Cinderella and Frou in disbelief.

"Frou may be old," said Cinderella, patting the horse's shaggy mane, "but he has the heart of a champion!"

The first thing Frou did, however, was trip over a nearby water trough. Cinderella flew over his head. She landed in the trough with a splash! The other horses whinnied with laughter, but Frou hung his head.

"Don't worry," Cinderella said to the King. "By next week, we'll be ready."

Cinderella and Frou trained for hours each day.

But Frou kept making mistakes. No matter how sweetly Cinderella urged him, he missed every jump.

And no matter how firmly she steered him, he went the wrong way every time.

"Oh, Frou," Cinderella said, patting his head, "I know you can do it!"

No one else was quite so sure – especially Frou!

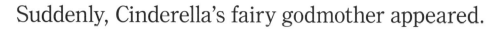

Suddenly, Cinderella's fairy godmother appeared.

"I overheard your little mouse friends talking," she explained.
"They said you need a miracle. So, here I am!"

Cinderella laughed and shook her head. "Oh, that's kind of you,"
she said. "But we don't need a miracle, just a good night's sleep."

"My dear," her fairy godmother whispered, "you know Frou
can win, and I know Frou can win, but our friend Frou
doesn't believe in himself yet. I'm going to help."

With that, she raised her magic wand and
waved it at Frou.

Suddenly, Cinderella and Frou had new outfits! A glass horseshoe appeared on each of Frou's hooves!

"With these horseshoes, you'll never miss a step," the Fairy Godmother said.

The next day at the horse show, Cinderella saw more fine horses than she had ever seen before. They all looked like champions – but so did Frou! He held his head up high and stamped his hooves proudly.

The King could hardly believe that Frou was the same horse he'd been watching trip and stumble all week long.

Frou cleared every jump with ease. He never took an awkward step or a wrong turn. He even managed a graceful little bow to the judges at the end of his routine.

Cinderella smiled. Her fairy godmother had been right. Frou had only needed a reason to believe in himself.

In the end, there was no question who belonged in the winner's circle – Princess Cinderella and Frou!

"You know," the King told the Grand Duke, "I had a special feeling about that horse all along...."

After the horse show, Frou returned to his stall at the palace stable with his head a little higher, his back a little straighter, and his glass shoes ready for the next time duty called.

The End

Beauty and the Beast
The Friendship Invention

"Oh, Papa, isn't it exciting?" Belle asked. She and her father, Maurice, were walking towards the centre of town. It was the day of the first annual Invention Convention. Maurice had been organizing it for months. And the big day had finally arrived!

"It certainly is," said Maurice. "People from all over the countryside are coming. I have a feeling there are some big surprises in store!"

When Belle and her father arrived, the town square was bustling with more activity than ever before! Townsfolk were eagerly setting up booths to present their incredible inventions.

"Why don't you go and explore while I get ready?" Maurice said.

Belle could hardly wait. She loved seeing new inventions. And there were so many on display!

Everywhere Belle looked there was a new imaginative contraption. Some had lots of bells and whistles. Others were quite practical. Some were simple and sweet.

Just when Belle thought she'd seen it all, she spied a crowd gathered across the square. Belle squeezed through the thick circle of people to see what everyone was oohing and ahhing over.

There must be something extra exciting over here, Belle thought.

When she reached the centre, Belle's eyes grew wide. In the
middle of the circle was an invention unlike any of the others. And the
inventor was a girl Belle's age! She was just about to demonstrate how
her machine worked, and she was looking for a volunteer.

"What's your name?" the girl asked Belle.

"I'm Belle."

"My name is Simone. Would you like to be my volunteer?" Simone guided Belle over to her invention. "Please place these leaves on the screen."

Belle did as she was asked. Then Simone closed the flap on the machine and pushed a button.

"*Et voilà!*" cried Simone.

Out popped one smooth little piece of paper. Simone's invention pressed tree leaves into paper! The crowd applauded.

As the people left, Belle helped Simone collect her pile of leaf paper.

"How did you think of such a clever invention?" Belle asked.

"When I was little, I always wanted to build an invention that could spread happiness," Simone explained. "One day I realized special notes make people happy. Sometimes you even make a new friend with a note. So I decided to invent a machine to create paper as special as the notes."

Belle looked at the stack of beautiful leaf paper. "That gives me a fantastic idea!" she said.

Simone look down at the paper, confused.

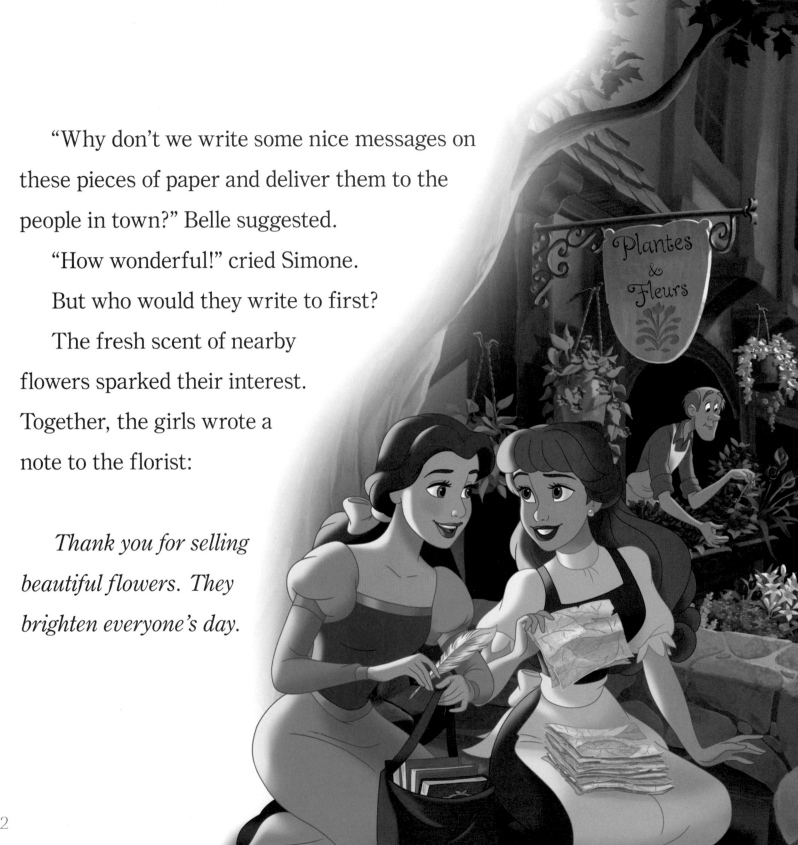

"Why don't we write some nice messages on these pieces of paper and deliver them to the people in town?" Belle suggested.

"How wonderful!" cried Simone.

But who would they write to first?

The fresh scent of nearby flowers sparked their interest. Together, the girls wrote a note to the florist:

Thank you for selling beautiful flowers. They brighten everyone's day.

132

Belle and Simone delivered the note, but they didn't sign it. They wanted to spread happiness in secret – that made it more exciting!

They watched as the florist opened his message. Reading it seemed to make him very happy!

"This is fun!" said Simone. "Let's write another one."

"Who should we write to next?" asked Simone.

Hmmm, Belle thought. "How about the bookseller? His books always make me happy. I think a nice note would be the perfect way to say 'thank you'."

So Belle and Simone wrote a note to the bookseller ...

... and delivered it in secret!

The bookseller was with a customer when he discovered it. Belle and Simone watched as he opened it, read it and smiled.

Belle winked. "Your invention is working!" she whispered to Simone. "It really is spreading happiness!"

Together, the girls delivered nice messages to many of the townsfolk. Soon they had only one sheet left.

"Who should we write our last note to?" Simone asked.

"I know just the person," said Belle.

A short while later, Belle and Simone delivered a very special handwritten message to Maurice. This time, they did not hide.

Dear Papa,

Thank you for organizing this wonderful convention. It brought two new friends together. – Belle and Simone

Maurice chuckled. "You're quite welcome." Then he handed the girls new books. "The bookseller asked me to give these to you. He recognized your handwriting, Belle, and wanted to thank you. The note made him very happy."

At the end of the day, the convention was over. It was time for Simone to pack up her invention and say goodbye.

"I had a wonderful time," Simone told Belle. "I'm so glad we met. And I wanted to give you this." She handed Belle a beautiful fresh stack of leaf paper. "Promise you'll write?"

Belle hugged Simone. "Of course," she said. "And you must write back to me. I want to hear about all the incredible new inventions you come up with!"

Belle waved as Simone's cart rolled away.

She was going to miss her new friend.

But later that night, when Belle opened her new book, she was surprised to find a special note from Simone tucked inside. And when she read it, she knew their friendship would last.

Belle couldn't wait to see Simone again. She was sure their next adventure would be even more fun.

Disney PRINCESS

Snow White
and the Seven Dwarfs

The Great Jewel Hunt

"Farewell, my love!" said Snow White. The Prince was leaving on a royal trip. It was the first time the newlyweds would be apart.

"I'll be home soon," replied the Prince. "In the meantime, I've left an envelope for you on the well. It's the first clue in a treasure hunt. At the end, you'll find a special gift!"

The clue was in plain sight. The Dwarfs gathered around as Snow White opened the envelope. "I wonder what the gift will be?" she said. Then she read the clue aloud:

Can't leave you a kiss,
Or even a hug,
So here is a clue:
Look under the ...

"I know!" cried Sneezy. "The Prince left the next clue under a bug!" Sneezy quickly led everyone to the garden.

Snow White and the Dwarfs looked under ladybirds, spiders, butterflies, beetles and, very carefully, bumblebees. But they didn't find a thing.

"Actually, it would be pretty hard to hide a clue under a bug," said Snow White. "Maybe it's hidden under something that sounds like bug?"

"Under a jug?" suggested Happy.

"No, he must have meant under a mug!" said Grumpy. "To the kitchen!"

But as the Dwarfs searched inside, Grumpy tripped over Dopey.

"Crawling on the floor in someone's castle is mad banners," scolded Doc. "I mean, it's very bad manners!"

"Whatever are you doing, Dopey?" asked Snow White.

Dopey crawled out from under the carpet and held up an envelope.

Snow White clapped her hands with excitement. "Under the *rug*! Oh, Dopey, you're a genius!"

Snow White read the clue:

Hooray, you found it! Easy when you try.
Now in the kitchen, just lift up the ...

"Pie!" shouted all of the Dwarfs at the same time. Searching had given them quite an appetite!

Sure enough, the next clue was hidden underneath the pie plate! First Snow White served everyone a big piece of freshly baked gooseberry pie. Then, while they were eating, she read the next clue.

Put on a smile, it's no time to frown.
You'll find the next clue in your royal ...

Snow White thought for a moment. "My royal gown?" she guessed. The Dwarfs all nodded in agreement and quickly finished off their pie.

In Snow White's dressing room, the Dwarfs searched through gown after gown after gown. But there was no clue to be found.

"Now we'll never find Snow White's gift," Sneezy said sadly.

Grumpy noticed Bashful standing in the corner. "Why aren't you searching?" Grumpy asked him.

"Why, he doesn't have to," Snow White said. "He's wearing my royal crown. That must be where the clue is!"

Bashful took off the crown ... and inside was the clue!

The gift is almost yours.
My, my, this game has flown!
There's one thing left to do:
Go look upon your ...

"Stone!" offered Sneezy.

"That's silly," said Grumpy.
"It must be bone!"

Soon all of the Dwarfs were shouting out their own ideas.

"Cone!"

"Cologne!"

"Trombone!"

To everyone's surprise, the birds flew down and placed a delicate
necklace around Snow White's neck. The gift was a stunning
heart-shaped ruby on a golden chain.

"Why, it's the colour of love," she said.

Doc saw that Snow White was holding something else. "The birds left a note!" he cried.

Snow White opened the envelope and read aloud:

Yes, jewels are lovely,
But as this hunt ends,
Keep one thought in mind:
The best gifts are ...

"Odds and ends," said Sneezy.

"No, it's definitely chickens and hens," said Happy.

"Pens?" Bashful suggested quietly.

Grumpy couldn't believe his ears. "What's wrong with you fellas? The answer is 'friends'!"

"You're right," said Snow White. "I love my new necklace, but the best part of today was the time we spent together. Friends are the greatest gift of all!"

All the Dwarfs cheered. Not even Grumpy could argue with that.

The End